For Ben and Tom, with love
–J.R.

For Ethan, who surprised
everyone by being so early
–T.W.

tiger tales
an imprint of ME Media, LLC
202 Old Ridgefield Road, Wilton, CT 06897
Published in the United States 2005
Originally published in Great Britain 2005
By Little Tiger Press
An imprint of Magi Publications
Text copyright ©2005 Julia Rawlinson
Illustrations copyright ©2005 Tim Warnes

Library of Congress Cataloging-in-Publication Data

Rawlinson, Julia.
A surprise for Rosie / by Julia Rawlinson ; illustrated by Tim Warnes.
  p. cm.
  Summary: Rosie Rabbit goes out exploring to discover the surprise that
Daddy Rabbit says he has for her.
  ISBN 1-58925-046-X (hardcover)
  [1. Rabbits—Fiction. 2. Surprise v Fiction.] I. Warnes, Tim, ill. II. Title.
PZ7.R1974Su 2005
[E]—dc22

2004017269

A Surprise for Rosie

by Julia Rawlinson

Illustrated by Tim Warnes

tiger tales

Rosie liked to know everything about everything, but Daddy Rabbit was planning a special surprise. Rosie kept trying to guess what it could be, but Daddy Rabbit only smiled and said, "Wait and see."

But Rosie couldn't wait.
While the other rabbits were
napping one afternoon, she
hopped out of the burrow.

Rosie hopped across
the stream, up the hill,
and through the meadow.

Brushing buttercups,
over the clover, under
the sun she hopped.
Around the big tree,
past a small tree, and
over a log she hopped.

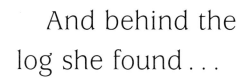

And behind the
log she found . . .

a bunch of acorns hidden
in a fallen hollow tree.

"That's not your surprise," chattered a
scampering squirrel.

"Do you know what my surprise is?" asked
Rosie, bouncing up and down.

"Yes. It's shaped a little bit like an acorn,"
said the squirrel. Then he scampered off with
some twigs, and Rosie hopped on.

She asked the butterflies and the
bees if they'd seen her surprise.
She asked the sheep and the cows
if they had seen it.

She asked the mice and
the moles if they had seen it.
And as she was asking the
moles she saw...

a secret entrance to the moles' tunnel.

"That's not your surprise," snuffled
the burrowing moles.

"Do you know what my surprise is?"
asked Rosie,
hopping around.

"Yes, we do. It's not a tunnel, but you can go into it," said the moles. Then they burrowed off to work on their tunnels.

Rosie searched under stones
and snail shells and bits of twig.
She searched through the dappled
sunshine of the forest.

She searched among the
scraggly tangles of the brush.
And in the brush she found . . .

a nest full of blue eggs.
"That's not your surprise,"
chirped Mommy Bird.

"Do you know what my surprise is?"
asked Rosie, sniffing the breeze.
"Yes. It's blue, a little bit like our eggs,"
said Daddy Bird as he fluttered to the nest.

Rosie hopped along, up a steep hill. She found a stone shaped like an acorn, but that wasn't her surprise. She found a fern-covered den that she could go into, but that wasn't the surprise, either.

She found a flower as blue as
a bird's egg, but that wasn't it.
Where could her surprise be?
Rosie stood up on her tiptoes.
She looked out over the
woods and . . .

tumbled down,
down, down the hill.
Rosie rolled head-over-heels.
Bumpity-bump, up in the air and
down on her tail fell Rosie. Slipping and
sliding, skidding and skittering, with four paws
flying, she tumbled.

Rosie finally landed in a heap, with a bump and a thud and a last little thump.

Then she sat up, twitched her ears, and gave a sad little sniff. "I'm never going to find this thing," she said, brushing dirt from her fur. "I'm tired of looking and hopping," she said, rubbing her bumped bunny nose.

"Too tired for your surprise?"
asked Daddy Rabbit, hopping up.
"Come with me and see..."

"your huge blue balloon of a surprise!
Jump in and ride with me."

"Ooh! Thank you, thank you!" said
Rosie, jumping in.

"Now I can see the whole wide world! I can see . . ."

"EVERYTHING!"